SORREL
The Substitute

Home Farm Twins

Sorrel
The Substitute

Jenny Oldfield

Illustrated by Kate Aldous

*Hodder
Children's
Books*

a division of Hodder Headline plc

A Catalogue record for this book is available from the British Library

ISBN 0 340 69984 1

Typeset by Avon Dataset Ltd, Bidford-on-Avon, Warks

Printed and bound in Great Britain by
Clays Ltd, St Ives plc

Hodder Children's Books
a division of Hodder Headline plc
338 Euston Road
London NW1 3BH

One

'Now, I'd like you all to listen very carefully!' Miss Wesley's low voice sang out across the sunny room. The top class of Doveton Junior were dozing their way towards the end of afternoon school.

Half-term holiday. *One whole week without lessons!* Hannah Moore told herself. Thursday to Thursday. Seven days of bliss.

Taking Speckle for walks, riding Solo up the fell . . . Helen Moore leaned forward, rested her head on her arms, shut her eyes, and began to daydream.

. . . Feeding the geese and hens at Home Farm, snuggling up with Socks, their cat, in a sunny windowsill . . . Sighing, Hannah gazed out of the window at the steep slopes of Doveton Fell.

. . . Mucking out, helping their dad to mend fences, paint doors, rebuild the rabbit run . . . Helen remembered the empty hutch and opened her eyes. Until a couple of months earlier, that hutch had been occupied.

'As you know, today is the last day of school before the half-term holiday,' Miss Wesley went on. She walked down the aisle between Helen and Hannah's desks, trailing a cloud of perfume. 'And it's time to decide who should look after Sage for the week.'

Hannah heard the name 'Sage' and dragged her attention back to what was going on inside the classroom. Of course, the school rabbit couldn't be left alone in an empty building. Someone would have to take him home and feed him . . . Who would that someone be? She glanced at Helen to see if she was wondering the same thing.

Helen flopped her dark, bobbed hair in front of her face and ignored Hannah. She'd sat up

straight now and had her gaze fixed on Miss
Wesley. For the first time she noticed what the
teacher had in her arms; it was a little ball of soft
black fur with long, pointed ears, pouchy cheeks
and big, dark eyes.

'Pay attention, Sam!' Miss Wesley came up
behind Sam Lawson and caught him napping in
the sunlight. 'I want to know who will look after
Sage while school is closed. You'll miss your
chance if you're not careful.'

The fair-haired boy from Crackpot Farm
shrugged. 'I've already got a rabbit of my own, so

I don't care!' he whispered to his neighbour.

'Now, put your hands up if you'd like to volunteer.' The teacher had arrived at the front of the class. She popped Sage into his hutch on a table by the window and quickly shut the wire-mesh door. He twitched his black nose, wiggled his whiskers and hopped lazily to his food dish.

'Me! Me! Me!' Half a dozen hands shot up.

'We will!' Hannah was quick off the mark. She jumped out of her seat, toppling her chair in her eagerness. 'We've got a spare hutch, Miss Wesley! We can look after Sage!'

'Sit down, Hannah.' The teacher hid a smile. 'How come your rabbit hutch is spare? Don't you have rabbits at Home Farm any more?'

'We did, but they dug their way out of the run we built. They escaped. Now there's no one living in the hutch!'

Helen groaned. *Wrong thing to say, Hannah!*

'I wouldn't let them look after Sage, Miss!' Sam Lawson jumped straight in. 'If they can't keep their own rabbits safe, I wouldn't trust them with this one!'

Hannah sat down with a thump. Helen glared

at Sam. He would say that, wouldn't he? Though he lived at the farm next door to the twins, they weren't exactly the best of friends.

'Hmm.' Miss Wesley surveyed the bunch of waving hands, giving Hannah and Helen a kindly, never-mind-Sam smile. 'I'm sure it was an accident that Hannah and Helen's rabbits escaped. Rabbits can dig their way out of practically any run. We can hardly blame the twins for that.' She went on with the task of selecting the right volunteer.

'Miss, choose me, Miss!' Lorna Milne pleaded.

'I thought your family was going to Devon for the week?'

'Oh . . . yeah, I forgot!' Crestfallen, Lorna's hand went down.

'Me, Miss!' Sam's friend, Mark Wood, put in his bid.

'What about your asthma, Mark? Didn't your mother tell me that animals make it worse?'

'Oh . . . yeah!' His face fell, he blushed.

One by one the volunteers dropped out. But Hannah kept her hand firmly in the air. They weren't going anywhere for the holiday, and they didn't have asthma, or grandmas who hated animals and had no garden. Their dad would mend the rabbit run and make it escape-proof. Sage would love it at Home Farm with Speckle the dog, Socks the cat, Solo the pony – a farmyard full of animals that had come to live with the Moores since they'd taken over the Lake District farm.

'. . . Well, Hannah, it looks like there's only you left!' Miss Wesley had come round to her at last.

Hannah's brown eyes nearly popped out of her head with the effort of hoping. *Choose me!* she'd chanted silently, following the teacher's slim figure from desk to desk. And her wish had come true.

'You're sure your mum won't mind taking in an extra lodger for the week? Perhaps we'd better ring her at the cafe to make sure.' Barbara Wesley was friendly with the twins' mother, Mary Moore, who ran the Curlew Cafe in nearby Nesfield.

'Mum won't mind, honest! Will she, Helen?' Hannah turned for support.

Helen shook her head. She was still gazing at Sage inside his hutch. Sure, he was sweet and fluffy. His long ears were lined with soft pinky-white fur, his black body was a round ball with a little powder-puff tail.

But he wasn't as sweet as the rabbits who had escaped; one pure white, one grey and brown speckled. Now, those rabbits had had *character*! They were cheeky and curious, friendly and adventurous. They didn't sit at the food dish all day chomping oats. She didn't have anything against Sage, but he did look . . . kind of boring.

'And what about your dad?' Miss Wesley wanted to make double sure.

'Dad won't even notice!' Hannah declared. He would be too busy taking photographs and developing them up in his attic dark-room. That was his job: selling animal and wildlife photographs to magazines, which he did from home.

The teacher was finally convinced. 'That's settled, then. Sage goes to Home Farm for the week!'

'Yes!' Hannah clenched her fist in triumph.

Sam Lawson muttered and grumbled. 'Something will go wrong, you watch! Their place is stuffed with animals. You can't move for them.

What do they need an extra one for?'

He and his friend, Mark, tagged after the twins as they carried Sage's hutch across the playground when the final bell had gone.

'You're just jealous, Sam!' Hannah retorted. At the school gate she could hear Miss Wesley checking arrangements with their dad.

'Yeah, yeah! I've got my own rabbit, like I said. A black Dwarf Dutch one like this, as a matter of fact.'

'Then stop moaning,' Helen put in. The rabbit hutch was heavy, and their teacher was still explaining things to their dad.

As Sam and Mark drifted off, forecasting disaster for the school rabbit, the twins rested the hutch on the ground. They peered in at Sage and listened to Miss Wesley's instructions to their dad.

'Plenty of fresh water; that's the main thing. In weather like this, when it's hot and sunny, a rabbit can quickly dehydrate. And here's a bag of Sage's favourite food pellets. They're a mixture of oats and other cereals. He's quite a fussy eater. He likes carrots and boiled potatoes too.'

David Moore took the food. 'Cordon Bleu

cooking for rabbits, eh? He wouldn't get fed like this if he came to live with us full-time.' The twins' dad teased and pretended that Sage was one spoiled rabbit. 'I suppose he's expecting five-star accommodation too?'

Inside his hutch, Sage thumped his back feet on the wooden floor.

Miss Wesley smiled. 'He can stay in his own little house if you like, though from what I remember, the hutch at Home Farm is pretty luxurious.'

'Specially designed and built!' the twins' dad said proudly. 'Just call me the DIY king of Doveton!'

Hannah raised her eyebrows. She recalled the help and advice they'd given as their dad built the hutch out of wood they'd rescued from a skip. 'No, Dad, that bit doesn't go there, it goes here!' They'd studied the plan and set him right. In the end, when they'd put it into position under the big horse-chestnut tree, it had looked *something* like the one in the book.

'Well, I'm obviously teaching my grandmother to suck eggs!' Miss Wesley laughed. 'There's nothing you don't know about looking after rabbits, is there?' She stood to one side and let Helen and Hannah pick up the hutch to carry it to the car. 'Oh, there is just one thing!'

They turned and listened.

'Give Sage plenty of exercise, otherwise I'm afraid he'll put on weight.'

'Will do! We'll mend the old run and pop him in there,' David promised, waving and getting into the car.

'And tell Mary I'll come up to Home Farm to see her this weekend!' Miss Wesley called. 'It's ages since we had a chat!'

Two

'Oh no, you don't, Socks! This is *Sage*'s dish of food!' Hannah shooed the greedy young cat away.

Helen took the bowl of diced vegetables from the kitchen table out into the farmyard. 'Whoever heard of a cat who liked carrots?'

Socks ran after her and wove between her legs as she walked across the stone flags, scattering chickens and geese as they went. The brown hens clucked, Lucy and Dandy the geese cackled, while from across the yard came the sound of hammering.

'Ouch!' their dad yelled. His thumb had got in

the way of the hammer. '*Thud-ouch, thud-ouch, ouch!*'

Out of sight, Speckle barked in sympathy.

Hannah grinned. 'That's Dad and Speckle mending the rabbit run in Solo's field. Do you think I'd better go and help?'

Helen nodded. 'If we plan to use it before Christmas, I think you better had!'

So Hannah split off and left Helen to feed Sage. It was their first evening of looking after the rabbit and they needed the run ready for the next morning. At this rate, it was never going to happen.

'It's OK, I can manage perfectly well, thank you!' David Moore's protests drifted over the stone wall and under the chestnut tree to where Helen approached Sage's hutch. 'Anyone would think I'd never attempted anything like this before!'

Helen smiled to herself. Their dad really fancied himself as an odd-job man, even though the bookcases he made fell to pieces and the hooks he'd put on the backs of the doors fell down as soon as you hung anything on them. Hannah would have her work cut out persuading him to make the old rabbit run escape-proof, she knew.

But meanwhile, she too had work to do. Sage had smelled food and was thumping up and down his hutch, kicking out with his strong back legs and churning up the layer of wood chippings on the floor. 'Hold your horses,' Helen told him, as she flipped the safe catch that held the wiremesh door in place.

Quick as a flash Sage saw a gap and shot straight for the exit. Hannah popped the dish in place, drew out her hand and pushed the door shut just in time. This rabbit wasn't as docile as he looked, she decided. There had been a certain look in his eye when he spotted the route to freedom which meant they had all better watch out.

'Did you see that?' she exclaimed, checking her hand and shaking it as her mum came out of the house and over towards the hutch.

'Formula One rabbit?' Mary Moore was just back home from the Curlew Cafe after another busy day. She'd taken the news of their unexpected guest in her stride, then brushed out her long, dark hair and changed into a T-shirt and shorts. 'He looked pretty speedy to me. What did you do to your hand?'

'Just grazed it on the wooden door-frame. It's OK, it doesn't hurt.' Helen watched Sage pick up a slice of carrot, hold it between his two front paws and crunch into it with his long front teeth. 'Do you think his hutch needs cleaning out?' she asked.

'Not tonight,' her mum answered. 'No, definitely not. Leave it until tomorrow, when he's settled in better.' She glanced up at the fresh green canopy and creamy-pink, candle-shaped blossoms of the tree. 'I thought I'd take Speckle for a walk up the lane. Do you want to come?'

So they went and rescued the Border collie from the stresses and strains of helping to repair the wooden frame that would form the five metre long run where Sage would get his exercise for the week. It was built in the shape of a triangle, like a giant Toblerone, and covered in wiremesh. But the mesh had come apart from the frame at one end, and now David Moore had to nail it back into place.

'Come on, Speckle!' Helen invited him on the walk. It was a lovely sunny evening, a pink sky promising a fine day tomorrow. Hannah decided she would join them.

'Have all the animals been fed?' their dad mumbled, a bunch of nails clenched between his teeth.

'Yep,' Helen said.

'Have you groomed Solo?'

'Yep.' Hannah had done it first thing after school.

'Have you collected the eggs?'

'Yep, yep, yep!' The twins vaulted the wall and began to run up the lane. Speckle streaked ahead while their mum ambled behind. Despite the usual chaos, all the chores had been done. Now all they need do was relax and dream of the holiday ahead.

'There you are, good as new!' Early next morning David Moore showed Helen and Hannah the mended run. He'd carried it into the yard for inspection.

'Brilliant, Dad!' Helen hardly stopped to look.

'Better than brilliant,' he insisted. There was tape wrapped around his bruised fingers, a look of pride on his face.

'Excellent!' Hannah rushed by without a second glance. She was carrying a scraper and a bucket to clean out Sage's hut. 'You reach in and lift him out,' she told an anxious Helen. 'Hold him while I get all this old bedding out!'

'Bye, girls!' Mary Moore called from the Curlew van as she set off for work.

Silence. Hannah and Helen were too busy to reply. Instead, Speckle and Socks trotted to the gate to watch her off down the hill.

'Got him?' Hannah asked.

Helen opened the hutch door a fraction and squeezed her arms inside. She could see Sage crouched in the far corner, his nose wrinkled, his whiskers twitching. Holding her breath, she inched her hands towards him, then clasped him tight. His strong back legs pedalled as she lifted him clear of the hutch. 'Quick, Hannah,' she urged. 'I don't know how long I can hang on to him!'

So Hannah moved in to scrape the floor of the hutch clean. Then she scrubbed it with disinfectant, dried it with a cloth and began to spread fresh chippings.

Helen held her breath. She had two and a half kilos of quivering rabbit in her arms. 'Shh!' she

said softly. 'No one's going to hurt you. We're just cleaning your hutch to make you comfortable!'

Sage shifted then settled in the crook of her arm. He snuffled at Helen's sweatshirt and licked her hand.

'That's better!' The rabbit had stopped quivering. She could tickle his head between his ears and see him begin to enjoy it. 'He's quite tame really, when you get to know him!'

'How about trying him out in the run?' Their dad had followed them across the yard, anxious to put his repair work to the test.

Helen cuddled Sage and glanced at Hannah. 'What do you think?'

'Just for a bit,' she agreed. 'But we'll have to keep watch. What time did we say we'd see Laura?'

'Half-nine.' Helen remembered that they'd arranged to take Solo out on the fell and meet up with their friend, Laura Saunders, and her horse, Sultan. She was happy that they'd been up early and given Sage everything a rabbit could need: more food, clean water, fresh bedding and tender loving care. All he needed now was the exercise that Miss Wesley had reminded them about.

'Come on, what are we waiting for?' David Moore strode back to the run and told Hannah to grab one end. 'Let's carry it back into the field and set it down on a nice flat stretch. Then Helen can put the rabbit inside and you two can go off for your morning's ride!'

'Will you be in?' she asked, frowing slightly.

'All day!' her dad insisted. 'Don't worry, I'll keep an eye on him!'

'Because he can be a bit frisky,' Helen warned,

carrying Sage carefully into the pony's field. Solo spotted them but kept his distance, ears pricked, staring at the contraption of wood and wiremesh that was invading his patch.

'Not him; he's just a little softie!' David Moore insisted, choosing his spot. He fixed the run nice and firm on the grass and began hammering in metal prongs like giant tent hooks to fix it to the ground.

Helen stroked the rabbit's shiny fur. 'This is just a con trick,' she warned her dad. There had been that look in Sage's eye last night when he'd leaped for freedom.

'To lull me into a false sense of security?' Her dad laughed and bent over to open a trap-door at one end of the run. 'I don't believe it. How can a cuddly little chap like him turn nasty?'

'Not nasty.' She knelt and popped the rabbit into the run. 'But he has a mind of his own, Dad. You'll need to keep watch!'

'Yes, yes, yes!' David Moore shooed them away. 'He'll be perfectly happy in there, you'll see.'

For a few minutes they watched Sage hop up and down the length of the run. He bobbed and sniffed, nibbled and grazed, scampered and braked when he came up against the wiremesh ends.

Helen hovered. Hannah hesitated.

'Go on !' their dad insisted. 'Or you'll be late!'

So they went. Solo was saddled, Speckle called, the bike brought out of the barn. It was half past nine and they were off, riding out to meet Laura and Sultan, knowing in their bones that leaving Sage out in the rabbit run was exactly the wrong thing to do!

'Where's he gone?' Helen cycled ahead of Hannah into Solo's field. They'd been away two hours, worrying about the rabbit every second they were out. Now, as she opened the gate, she saw that the run was empty.

'Dad must have put him back in his cage,' Hannah decided. She felt her heart thump as she dismounted and ran with Speckle into the yard.

'No!' Hannah got there ahead of her. 'He hasn't!'

'Are you sure Sage isn't asleep?' There was a sleeping compartment in a gallery made of wood, completely shut off from the daylight.

Hannah peered through the small doorway. 'I can't see him!' Her voice had risen to a squeak. Where could he be?

'Dad, where's the rabbit?' Helen sprinted for the house, yelling at the top of her voice. 'Dad! Dad! What have you done with Sage?'

He came to the door, a roll of film in his hand, his wavy brown hair untidy as it always was when he concentrated hard on his work. 'Me? I haven't done anything with him,' he muttered.

'He's vanished. Come and help us look!' Hannah veered off towards the field once more. She was down on her hands and knees examining the empty run when the others caught her up.

'He can't have vanished, he must be somewhere . . .' David Moore frowned and scratched his head. 'I checked him just ten minutes ago.'

Helen sped to the far end of the run and gasped. She pushed an inquisitive Speckle out of the way. 'Come and look at this!'

Hannah's heart sank. She saw in an instant what Helen was pointing at: a neat heap of loose earth, and a hole under the wooden border of the run just wide and deep enough for a determined little rabbit to squeeze clean through!

Three

'Don't tell Miss Wesley!' Helen pleaded with David Moore, as soon as they realised it was true. They'd searched Solo's field from top to bottom, and there was still no sign of Sage.

Hannah too wanted to keep the guilty secret. 'We're sure to find him sooner or later!' she insisted.

'Even if we have to look all day!'

'And all night!'

'We'll bribe him back into his hutch with food!'

'We'll get Speckle to follow his trail!'

The twins were desperate for their dad not to

let the teacher know. 'Honestly, Dad, it'll get us into serious trouble if you tell her,' Helen begged.

David Moore shook his head. 'It might be better to own up and get it over and done with.' He'd made the girls go into the house for lunch after they'd searched for Sage for more than an hour. 'Barbara will understand. She knows that these things can happen.' He gave them a chunky cheese sandwich and made them eat. 'I can tell her it was my fault. After all, I was in charge of the rabbit when it made its getaway.'

'But she'll never trust us again!' Hannah hated the idea of letting their teacher down.

'And Sam Lawson will laugh at us.' Helen muttered savagely through a mouthful of bread and cheese. 'He'll say "I told you so!"'

'And he did!' Hannah groaned. 'Come on, let's take Speckle and keep on looking.' She stood up from the kitchen table, scraping her chair on the stone flagged floor. 'Give us time, Dad. There's no need to tell yet, is there?'

Looking at their anxious faces, their dad nodded. 'But I should warn you that looking for Sage will be a bit like hunting for a needle in a haystack by this time. After all, he's got a couple of hours start on you already. He could be anywhere: up on the fell, down in the village, in any of the farmyards round here . . .'

Hannah and Helen heard his voice fade into the background as they ran out into the farmyard. Then Helen turned and dashed back in.

'. . . He could have dug a burrow and vanished down it, or reached the cover of some nice dark barn where you would never find him.'

'Carrots!' Helen cried. She ignored her dad and scrabbled in the vegetable rack.

'Pardon?'

'Carrots! Sage likes carrots. We can use them to tempt him back home!' Quickly she grabbed two juicy specimens and dashed out to join Hannah.

'I've shown Speckle the empty hutch,' Hannah gasped. She had the dog on the lead, ready to pick up the search where they'd left off. 'He knows we're still looking, and he's got Sage's scent!'

So they began with the barn in their own farmyard, letting Speckle loose to sniff at the doorposts, looking into dark corners where they kept Solo's tack and feed, rummaging behind their dad's big box of tools and stacks of spare wood.

'Anything?' Helen whispered. Speckle was still zig-zagging across the entrance, nose to the ground. Hannah was up in the hay loft, shining a torch with one hand, holding out a carrot in the other.

'Not yet.' Hannah peered behind bales of straw. 'Here, Sage! That's a good rabbit. Nice, juicy carrot. Come along!' She made tweeting noises with her lips to encourage him in case he was frightened.

Suddenly Speckle shot off across the farmyard towards the gate. The white flash of his tail bobbed eagerly as he went.

'He's found something! He's picked up a scent!' Helen called for Hannah to come down quick. She followed the dog, who had squeezed under the gate into the lane alongside Solo's field.

Soon Hannah joined her, to find the border collie already rooting in the overgrown ditch.

'Good boy, Speckle!' Helen jumped in after him, tangling her legs in the brambles, glad that she was wearing jeans. The water in the ditch sucked and oozed around her trainers, but she didn't care; Speckle was on the trail!

But then he was up and out of the ditch, criss-crossing the narrow lane, sniffing hard.

Helen clambered out, squelching her feet back on firm ground. 'False alarm!' she sighed. When she thought about it, Sage was hardly likely to take refuge in a muddy ditch.

'No, look! Speckle's still picking up the trail!' Hannah watched him take a new course, across the lane again, between some old stone gateposts and down the track to Crackpot Farm.

Hannah gasped and stopped. 'Don't say Sage chose Sam Lawson's farm to hide in!' Here, of all places. When he could have chosen anywhere, from the wide open hillsides to the trees that lined Doveton Lake.

'We'll never live it down,' Helen agreed, quickly stuffing the carrots into her back pocket as she spotted Sam set off down the lane on his bike to meet them.

He arrived with a squeal of brakes and a cloud of dust. 'What are you up to? What have you lost?'

He stared suspiciously at Speckle, who had taken a detour into a nearby field.

'Nothing!' they said, in the same breath.

'We're picking blackberries!' Helen gabbled.

'It's too early in the year.' Standing astride his bike, Sam narrowed his eyes.

'Sorry, I meant strawberries!' This only made it worse, she knew.

'*Wild* strawberries!' He looked at her as if she was mad. 'They don't grow round here, in case you didn't know.' Sam meant to make them painfully aware that they'd come to Doveton after living all their lives in a town.

'Anyway, gotta go!' Hannah cut in. Speckle had made off across country and disappeared in amongst some tall ferns. So far, he'd sniffed eagerly and run ahead as if he knew exactly which way Sage had gone. But there hadn't been a sign of a single whisker or the tip of a long black ear.

'Mad!' Sam watched them follow the dog with a shake of his head. He cycled back up the lane.

'Do you think he suspected anything?' Helen dropped to her hands and knees to crawl through the ferns. She could see Speckle up ahead, still concentrating on the trail.

'Oh, no!' Hannah tossed her fringe out of her eyes and crawled alongside. 'Not a thing!' She began to think their dad was right; finding the runaway rabbit was an impossible task.

But they carried on, right through the afternoon, as the sun began to sink behind the fell, throwing long shadows and bringing out wild rabbits from their burrows in the quiet hollows and shady woods. Out they hopped: pale brown, silent creatures with long, white ears and bobbed tails. Big and small, solitary or in groups of five or six, they came to graze and sit in the evening sun.

'Not a black one in sight!' Hannah whispered. She sat on a high rock with her arm around a tired Speckle, to keep him from chasing the tempting creatures. Together they looked down on the peaceful scene.

'They wouldn't let Sage down one of their burrows, anyway.' Helen knew that wild rabbits wouldn't mix with a tame one. 'If he's got any hope of staying alive out here, it'll be by finding a warm, dry place in a farm shed or a barn, like Dad said.'

It was the first time that either of them had mentioned the danger poor Sage might be in. Hannah shuddered. It was getting cold. 'Shall we go back home?' she asked quietly.

Helen nodded. 'Maybe Sage never came this far after all.' They set off down the steep hill, beside a fast-running stream. 'Speckle could have picked up the wrong scent.'

Glancing down at the tired dog, Hannah shook her head. 'Not Speckle.'

For a while they walked in silence. Then another thought struck Helen. 'Oh no!' she cried, and stopped dead.

'What?' Hannah's own heart thumped. She thought Helen had seen something awful on the shadowy path ahead.

'Miss Wesley! She said she'd come to see Mum this weekend!'

'Oh no!' Hannah echoed. 'So how long have we got?' She wracked her brains to remember exactly when the visit was due. This was even worse than they'd thought; if the teacher came for a friendly chat, she was bound to ask to see Sage – and what was there to show her now except an empty hutch?

'Come on!' Helen set off again at a run. 'We've got to stop her!'

'How?' Hannah kept up, urging Speckle into a lope beside them.

'I dunno. Let's say we've all got chicken pox or something!' Helen was desperate. 'Just to give us more time to get Sage back before she comes!'

Their legs ached and their lungs hurt as they scrambled over walls and ran across fields until they came to Home Farm.

Too late: their mum's van was in the yard, the door was open. She was chatting on the phone.

'That'd be great, Barbara. Come for tea tomorrow. I'll get off work early and we can have a nice long evening together . . . Yes, that's fine then. Bye!'

Helen and Hannah ground to a halt. They heard the words, 'Barbara . . . tea tomorrow.' Inside the house, their mum and dad carried on chatting.

'Twenty-four hours!' Hannah moaned.

'Don't panic!' Helen said, panicking anyway.

They had less than a day to find Sage. She turned this way and that, as if the runaway rabbit would show up like magic if she wished hard enough. She ran to look in the hutch again, just in case. Empty. So she turned to Hannah and grabbed her arm. 'What on earth are we gonna do now!' she hissed.

'Are you sure this is a good idea?' Helen asked, as they slipped quietly out of the house early next morning.

Hannah nodded. They hadn't told a soul about their plan; not their dad, and definitely not their mum. Mary Moore had insisted that they must tell Barbara Wesley the truth, the whole truth and nothing but the truth when she came for tea. 'Unless you find Sage before she arrives, of course. In which case, all will be well!'

That was their mum for you. She was cut and dried when it came to being honest, never let them get away with anything. So when she'd heard about Sage's great escape, she'd made them promise to tell the whole story.

'Do you really think we can trust Sam Lawson?'

Helen repeated her doubts. Their mum had gone off to work, their dad was up in his dark-room. Suddenly Hannah had come up with what she'd said was a brilliant idea.

'. . . I know!' Her face had lit up as she sat on the wall under the chestnut tree.

'What?' Helen had been reluctant to believe that Hannah had found a solution to the problem. She'd gone on sulkily feeding the hens.

'Let's ask Sam if we can borrow his rabbit for the day!'

'How do you mean, borrow?' Helen had curled her lip in disbelief.

'I mean, ask him if he'll lend us his black rabbit. He said he'd got one of his own, remember? And it's supposed to be a Dutch Dwarf rabbit, just like Sage. If we put Sam's rabbit in Sage's hutch, Miss Wesley would never notice the difference!'

Slowly Helen had seen how the plan might work. 'You mean, we swear Sam to secrecy. We don't tell Mum and Dad what we're doing. We just let them think we found Sage. But we didn't; not really. What we're doing is putting Sam's rabbit in his place. A substitute rabbit!'

34

'Just until Miss Wesley's been and gone!' Hannah had been convinced that it would work.

'. . . What if she notices?' Helen said over and over. She said it again now, as they swung open the gate to Crackpot Farm.

'She won't,' Hannah insisted. 'Black rabbits all look the same, unless you're another black rabbit, I expect.'

'But what if Sam won't agree to lend us his?' The doubts gnawed away at Helen as they approached the farm door.

'He will!' Hannah said firmly. 'Just you watch this!'

Four

'Hello, girls! This is a nice surprise!' Mrs Lawson greeted them as she climbed into the Land-Rover to drive into town. 'Sam's cleaning his bike round the back. He looks bored out of his mind already. He never knows what to do with himself during the school holidays, so I'm sure he'll be pleased to see you.'

'I'm not bored.' Sam appeared around the corner of the house as the car drove off.

'And not pleased to see us either, by the look of things,' Helen whispered. Sam was frowning at the cat basket which Hannah was carrying, and she was feeling more nervous than ever.

'Hi, Sam!' Hannah put on a breezy voice. She got straight to the point. 'We came to see your rabbit!'

'Sorrel?' His frown deepened. 'What for?'

'Sorrel?' She tried out the name. 'That's nice. We're just interested, that's all.' Hannah put the basket down under a bench, out of the way. Before she plunged in any deeper, Hannah had to be sure that Sam's rabbit was the same as Sage. She looked across the yard as they followed him round. 'Where do you keep the hutch?'

'Why do you want to know?' He answered each question with another question, casting suspicious looks from one to the other.

This will never work! Helen sighed to herself.

'There it is!' Hannah spied the hutch beside the shed where Sam kept his bike. She sped across to take a closer look.

'What's going on?' Sam asked a silent Helen.

'Look!' The excitement grew in Hannah's voice as she peered into the wooden hutch. There, sitting on its haunches, nibbling a lettuce leaf, was a small, round black rabbit with long pink ears and fat, pouchy cheeks. 'Identical!'

'Incredible!' Even Helen was impressed. The same big, almond-shaped brown eyes, the same snuffly black nose and long, tufted ears.

'Now, just a minute, you two!' Suddenly Sam clicked. He guessed what the twins had been searching for in the lane the day before, he knew why they'd come here now. '. . . The answer's no!'

'What did we say?' Hannah turned and tried to look as if she didn't know what he was talking about, opening her brown eyes wide, spreading her palms upwards.

'You didn't need to say anything! You've gone and lost the school rabbit and now you want to borrow Sorrel so no one finds out!'

'Just for today,' Hannah wheedled. She decided to confess everything. 'You can have Sorrel back tomorrow morning. Miss Wesley's coming to Home Farm for tea, so we just need a substitute for tonight. Can't we borrow your rabbit? Ple-ee-ase?'

'No.' Sam turned away with a shrug and began to polish the spokes on the back wheel of his mountain bike.

'I knew it!' Helen said gloomily. Back to square one. What on earth were they going to do now?

But Hannah hadn't finished yet. If pleading hadn't done the trick, perhaps a bribe would. 'How much?' she said boldly.

Sam stopped polishing. 'Fifty pence.' The answer came this time, quick as a flash.

'Done!' Before he could change his mind, Hannah dipped into her pocket for the coin.

Helen stared at Sam, who blushed.

'Well, it's only fair,' he protested. 'You're kind of hiring Sorrel from me, and I'm charging you.'

'It's fine, it's fine,' Hannah gabbled. 'Hold the door of the hutch open, Helen. Thanks, Sam. We'll take good care of Sorrel, don't worry.' She couldn't wait to pick up the rabbit and get out of there.

'And swear you won't tell?' Helen watched Hannah take Sorrel's weight and lift him out. She needed Sam's promise before she ran to fetch the cat basket.

''Course. I won't say a word.' His face stayed blank as he swore. 'If you keep Sorrel for longer, the charge goes up. It's fifty pence a day.'

'Robber!' Helen protested.

'Fine!' Hannah was on her way, snuggling Sorrel against her. She didn't care what Sam charged. She'd use her pocket money to pay him if Helen didn't want to. They'd got an identical rabbit to Sage, and that was the only thing that mattered.

'. . . Except, Sorrel's a little bit fatter than Sage,' Helen pointed out. They'd got him safely back to Home Farm. Now he was settled comfortably into Sage's empty hutch. They'd put him in there with fresh water and food, and slipped off with Speckle to continue the search for the real Sage. Meanwhile, their dad had spotted the new arrival and jumped to the wrong conclusion, as the twins had hoped.

'Well done, girls!' he'd cried. 'You found the rabbit. Where was he in the end?'

'Over at Crackpot Farm,' Hannah explained. She hadn't actually told a lie, after all.

Their dad had been pleased, but too busy to ask questions. The same with their mum, when she arrived home from work. 'Oh, that's good!'

She smiled at the black rabbit in the hutch. 'All that worry, and now Sage is back safe and sound. You'll be able to greet Barbara with a clear conscience after all.'

The twins smiled and said nothing until they were alone in the farmyard.

'It's working!' Hannah sighed. Little Sorrel hadn't seemed to mind being moved. When she'd taken him out of the cat basket and put him into the hutch under the chestnut tree, he'd sniffed in all the corners and slowly tested the ramp up into the sleeping quarters. He'd taken a nibble of oats from the dish and a drink of water from the bottle clipped to the wiremesh front. Then he'd taken a nap.

'It looks like we're going to get away with it,' Helen agreed. 'Mind you, Mum and Dad didn't look very closely at Sorrel. Miss Wesley's likely to be more interested.' The teacher would be here soon, and that would be the real test.

'Hmm.' Hannah studied the new rabbit. 'Sorrel *is* a bit fatter than Sage, I must admit.'

'We'll have to say we've been feeding him up.'

'But Miss Wesley said Sage had to have plenty

of exercise, remember? She doesn't like him to get too fat.'

They were in a huddle in front of the hutch, when their mum came out into the yard to hang up the washing.

'What are you two whispering about?' she asked, shaking wet towels from the tangle in the laundry basket and pinning them to the line.

'Nothing!' they chorused.

'Good, because there's plenty to do inside before Barbara gets here. Run and set the table for tea for a start.'

So they had to leave Sorrel napping and nibbling in his new hutch and get ready for their visitor. Plates, knives and forks were laid out on the table, home-made chocolate cake sliced and set in the middle, the kettle boiling by the time Miss Wesley's car pulled up in the yard.

'She's here!' Helen ran to the window and looked out. Their off-duty teacher wore a summer dress and sandals, her hair was loose and she carried a pot of busy lizzies as a present for their mum as she came into the kitchen.

Hannah showed Helen her crossed fingers.

There would be tea first, and knowing their mum, plenty of chat. Time to get even more nervous than she felt already. Then Miss Wesley was bound to ask them about Sage.

'. . . The cake was delicious. I don't know how you find the time.'

'. . . What about you? Teachers have to do so much preparation and marking these days, it's a wonder you have any time to yourself.'

The conversation drifted on, long after the teacups had been cleared. David Moore had popped his head round the door to say hello to Miss Wesley and given Helen and Hannah a kind wink, as if to say, 'Don't look so worried. Everything turned out fine in the end, didn't it?'

'And you've taken on all these animals,' Miss Wesley was saying now. She smiled as Socks stalked a ball of screwed-up paper across the kitchen floor and Speckle nosed it out of reach.

'The girls look after the animals,' Mary Moore explained. 'That's their job.' Just then, the telephone rang and she got up to answer it.

'Talking of looking after animals . . .' The teacher stood up and smoothed her dress. She turned to the twins. 'How's Sage?'

Hannah swallowed hard. This was it. 'Fine!' There was a squeak in her voice that she couldn't control.

'Where did you decide to keep him? Shall we take a look?'

As Hannah cleared her throat, Helen stepped in. 'This way.'

And before they knew it they were out in the yard, hearing the drying towels flap in the breeze, picking their way between the pecking hens, heading for the rabbit hutch under the tree.

'You chose a perfect spot!' Miss Wesley spied the hutch set on the stone ledge by the wall. 'Nice and high up, out of the way of mice and foxes and suchlike. I expect you get quite a lot of them on a farm.'

'A few.' Hannah didn't trust herself to say more. This was worse than any maths test Miss Wesley had ever set them. Every step towards the hutch seemed to take an age, wondering if the plan would work.

'And it's a very – er – sturdy hutch.' The teacher

searched for the right word for the little wooden house.

'Dad made it,' Helen told her. 'From old floorboards.'

'It certainly does the job.' She stooped to peer inside. 'It even has a separate sleeping compartment that cuts out the daylight. I'm impressed!'

Hannah and Helen came up on either side. They too peered into the hutch, hardly daring to breathe.

'Where's Sage? I suppose he must be asleep in there.' Miss Wesley had looked into every corner but not spotted the rabbit. She was ready to give up and go back to the house.

'No, here he is!' Helen saw a soft black nose push out of the door to the sleeping compartment, then a pair of long ears. She brought Miss Wesley back to look without stopping to think.

And then it was too late for Hannah to steer her away. The teacher turned, in time to see Sorrel hopping down the ramp. His shiny black coat was covered in bits of wood chipping, he wrinkled his nose and kept his eyes still half

closed in the sudden glare of daylight.

'My!' Barbara Wesley was taken aback. 'Is it my imagination, Sage, or have you grown?' She bent to peer more closely. 'I can see someone has been feeding you up!' she tutted. But she was smiling as she spoke. She put her fingers against the wire-mesh, reaching through to touch the rabbit's soft fur.

Sorrel turned and nuzzled at her finger, soaking up the attention.

'Can I lift him out?' the teacher asked.

Hannah nodded and opened up the hutch. So

far, so good. 'We're sorry if we've been giving him too much to eat,' she said, as she picked Sorrel up and handed him over.

'He weighs a ton!' Miss Wesley joked. 'We'll have to put you on a diet when we get you back to school, my boy!'

But she was happy to see that the rabbit looked content. She stroked him and fussed over him, and she didn't notice that Sage wasn't Sage, that this was Sam Lawson's Sorrel; a different rabbit completely.

'We did it!' Helen ran and told Speckle and Socks. She swept the cat into her arms, dandled him in the air and wriggled him to and fro.

'Shh!' Hannah warned. Their mum and dad were still waving Miss Wesley off after the successful visit.

'We did it!' Helen told Solo as she went to bring him in for grooming. 'Sorrel pretended to be Sage, and we got away with it. We did it!'

The evening drew in, blossom petals from the chestnut tree drifted in the breeze. Tomorrow they would take Sorrel back to Crackpot Farm and renew the search for Sage.

Hannah had stopped by the hutch as Helen led Solo across the yard. The little black rabbit had come alive in the cool of the evening. He hopped noisily up and down his cage, his back feet thumping. '*You* did it!' Hannah whispered to him. 'Without you, we'd never have stood a chance!'

Five

By Saturday morning, Sage, the real school rabbit, had been missing for a day and a half.

'Two nights and one day,' Hannah murmured sadly. She kept her voice down so that their mum and dad couldn't hear from the bedroom next door.

Helen pictured Sage out in the wild, trying to survive. 'I bet he's hungry,' she whispered.

'And scared.' Hannah slipped her feet into her trainers. 'Unless he's found a good place to hide.' This was her one hope. All night she'd been trying to convince herself that Sage had found a refuge

51

that would keep him safe from harm.

'Yes. Maybe that's why we haven't been able to track him down so far.' Helen too was up and dressed, though it was only just light. They were going to try again to find the runaway rabbit, and this time they were determined to succeed.

'We'll call in at Crackpot Farm and leave Sam a note if he's not up yet,' Hannah decided. 'Let's say we'll take Sorrel back at lunchtime.'

'And hope that we've got Sage back by then.' If not, Helen knew they would have a whole lot more explaining to do.

'We will.' Ever hopeful, Hannah went down-stairs, called Speckle and they set off to scour the fields and hills once more.

'Carrot-bait!' Helen produced the two limp vegetables from her pocket.

'Cat basket!' Hannah had thought it was best to take it just in case. It would be safer to bring Sage back in than carrying him in her arms.

'Bye, Sorrel!' Helen whispered as they sped past the hutch.

Sam's rabbit was already up and about, sitting

in the early sun, carefully plucking tufts of soft fur from his chest.

'Why's he doing that?' Hannah frowned. 'Doesn't it look strange to you?'

Helen shrugged. 'He's probably just grooming himself.' She noticed Sorrel carry the plucked tufts up the ramp into his sleeping compartment. 'Or making himself a comfy nest. Come on, let's go!'

They vaulted the wide gate into the lane, then crossed fields until they came to High Hartwell; Fred Hunt's dairy farm overlooking the green slopes down to Doveton Lake. By the time they got there, Fred had already had his black and white cows in for milking and was herding them back out on to the pasture.

'A black rabbit?' he asked, when Hannah explained what they were up to. He didn't sound surprised; but then Fred Hunt never did. 'Well, I haven't seen one. But I'll look out for him, now that I know you've lost him.' He gave the last cow in the queue a tap on her broad backside and urged her into the field.

'Thanks, Fred!' Helen ran on. Next they would try John Fox down at Lakeside Farm. These old farmers knew everything that was going on in the area. Even something as small as a black rabbit on the run would catch their attention.

But, 'No,' John Fox answered, scratching his head and whistling his sheepdog, Ben, back from penning half a dozen sheep in a fold. 'I've not heard of this rabbit of yours. I'll let you know if I do.'

'Do you think Sage will be able to survive out here?' Hannah gazed up the hillside at the blobs of white against the green: John's sheep grazing far up the fell.

'Maybe.' The farmer shrugged. 'As long as he steers clear of this fox I've been seeing round here of a night time.'

'Fox?' The word froze Helen to the spot.

'Yes, if you ask me he's a real nuisance. He comes right into the yard here, kicks up an awful row amongst my hens. Bold as brass, he is. If I don't watch him, he'll have one of those chickens for his supper before too long!'

Hannah shivered. 'Would he eat a rabbit?' she asked quietly.

Mr Fox nodded. 'He'd consider that a tasty morsel if he could catch it.'

The new fear sent them chasing on, away from Lakeside Farm, into the village, and on a wide loop back up the hill, past Dan and Julie Stott's place at Clover Farm. Everywhere the answer was the same; 'No, we haven't seen your rabbit. But we'll let you know if we do.'

By lunchtime, Hannah and Helen arrived back home tired and dejected, and still no nearer to finding Sage.

'I've had a very strange message from Sam Lawson while you were out,' David Moore told them as soon as they walked into the house. He was loading film into his camera at the kitchen table. 'It didn't make any sense to me; something about another fifty pence that you owe him for the rabbit.'

Helen groaned. Trust Sam.

'He asked where you were, and I had to admit I didn't know exactly.' Their dad eyed them closely. 'So what have you two been up to?'

'Nothing much.' Hannah struggled to hide the disappointment she felt over Sage. And she was wondering whether they should pay Sam what he was asking and keep Sorrel for another day, when the phone rang.

'Get that, would you?' their dad said, as he wandered out, camera in hand.

Absent-mindedly Hannah picked it up and spoke their number.

'Hello. Is that Helen?' a voice asked.

'No, it's Hannah.'

'Oh, Hannah. It's Barbara Wesley here.' She was brisk and businesslike, as if she was already back at school. 'Listen, I've been into the village this morning and I picked up a lot of gossip about a fox. Have you heard?'

'Yes. It's been after the chickens at Lakeside Farm.'

'That's right. And the doves at Luke Martin's shop. Practically everyone in the village has a tale to tell about this particular dog-fox. It seems it's a big one, and very daring. It doesn't mind being spotted when it's out on a raid either; just carries on regardless unless one of the farmers sets his own dog on it. Anyway, I thought I'd better warn you.'

'Thank you.' A big, fierce dog-fox. Poor,

defenceless Sage out in the dark nights. She took a deep breath then sighed.

'What's wrong, Hannah?' Miss Wesley sounded concerned. 'You haven't seen it out your way, have you?'

'No. I don't think it's come this far. Speckle would have warned us if it had been near.' Out of the corner of her eye, she saw the dog wag his tail at the mention of his name.

'Oh yes, I'd forgotten about Speckle. Yes, that's good.' There was a pause before Miss Wesley went on. 'What I'm really trying to say, Hannah, is that I'm worried about Sage now that this fox is around. I'm even wondering if I should come up to Home Farm and fetch him down here to Watersmeet where I can keep an eye on him myself!'

'No, don't do that!' Hannah cried. That was the worst thing the teacher could possibly do.

'Well, if you keep a special eye on him for me instead, that should be all right. But don't let him out of the hutch, just in case.'

'We won't,' she promised.

'And if you have any problems, just give me a ring.'

'OK, thanks.' Quickly Hannah put down the phone.

'You've gone white,' Helen told her. 'You look like you've seen a ghost.'

'Oh, what are we going to do?' she wailed, slumping into a chair and leaning her elbows on the table. Everything was going wrong and there was nothing they could do about it. Now the picture of the fox with its long, dark snout and pointed teeth, creeping through the black night would haunt her every waking moment.

'How about getting a bus into Nesfield, going to a pet shop and trying to buy another black rabbit?' It was Helen's turn to be practical and admit that they would probably never find poor Sage now.

'And give up?' Hannah shook her head. 'We can't do that. What if Sage is still alive and trying to find his way back?'

'But, Hannah, we've looked and looked!'

'He can't just have vanished!'

Helen left a long pause, watching their dad come trotting back across the yard towards the house as if he had some news. 'Maybe Sage is already dead,' she said quietly.

Then David Moore burst into the kitchen. 'I thought you said this rabbit was a "he"!' he cried.

'It is. *He* is!' Hannah jumped up in alarm. *What now?*

'Well that's mighty peculiar!' Their dad was waving for them to follow him, heading back towards the gate.

Helen stared at Hannah. They both shrugged. Whatever it was, it must be pretty exciting. They followed after him.

'Come and look!' he cried. Then he stopped short of the hutch and held them back. 'Go slowly,' he ordered, dropping his voice to a whisper. 'We mustn't disturb them!'

'Them'? Had their dad gone mad? Gently they eased forward to peer into the hutch.

'Not there, here!' David Moore drew the twins away from the wiremesh and lifted a hinged section of the roof to let them peep into the sleeping compartment. As their eyes grew used to the dim light inside the box, they could make out a nest of wood chippings and soft black fur, and Sorrel sitting hunched and puffed out to one side.

'Can you see?' their dad whispered.

'What?'

'Where?'

Sorrel blinked up at them without moving.

'In the nest. Look again!'

'Oh!' Helen cried.

'Aah!' Hannah couldn't believe her eyes.

Curled up inside the nest, side by side, with their eyes closed, were six tiny, skinny baby rabbits.

Six

'Wait till I see Sam Lawson; I'll kill him!' Helen hissed. She'd got over the shock of discovering that chubby little Sorrel wasn't a 'he', but a 'she', and about to have babies when Sam had rented her out.

'Maybe he didn't know either.' Hannah looked for excuses, still amazed at how small and helpless the baby rabbits were. They slept in a heap of tiny limbs and hairless pink bodies while a proud Sorrel looked on.

'And there's another thing . . .!' Thoughts flashed into Helen's head as the surprise news sank in. 'If he thinks we're going to pay him fifty pence a day until these babies can be moved back to Crackpot Farm, he's got another think coming!'

'You mean we'll have to keep them here?' In spite of everything, Hannah glowed with pleasure.

'For days and days. Weeks even. Sorrel will need peace and quiet to feed the babies, won't she? She won't want to be disturbed.'

Hannah nodded, her eyes bright at the idea. 'And we thought she was just fat!' she giggled.

'We thought she was a he!' Helen reminded her. 'And that's Sam's fault!' He'd got them into a fine mess, now that their dad had rushed off to the phone to give Miss Wesley the good news.

Hannah closed the lid on the hutch. 'I suppose we'd better leave Sorrel alone for a bit.' She sighed and looked up, seeing with surprise the figure of Sam Lawson speeding down the lane on his bike.

'Just the person I want to talk to!' Helen said with menace. She strode to the gate to greet him.

'Helen, wait!' Hannah didn't want a row. She could tell by the fierce look in her sister's eye that Sam was riding straight into one. When Helen got mad, everyone had better watch out.

'Sam Lawson!' she began, climbing over the gate into the lane.

He braked and skidded to a halt. By the time Helen had vaulted and landed, he had flung his bike into the grass verge and stood hands on hips. 'I thought you said you were gonna bring Sorrel back after lunch!'

'So?' Helen demanded. Sam had taken the wind out of her own sails by getting in first.

'So, why didn't you wait?'

'What?'

'Why didn't you do what you said in the note? I expect it was so you wouldn't have to pay me another fifty pence, knowing you. Anyway, I wasn't in when you showed up with the rabbit, was I?'

'When we what?' Hannah stepped forward to sort out the muddle. She could see that Helen was baffled too.

'When you brought Sorrel back to Crackpot Farm, I wasn't in, was I?'

'But we . . .' Hannah frowned.

'. . . Didn't!' Helen finished off the sentence.

Sam snorted. 'Don't give me that. 'Course you did!'

'No, honestly, we haven't been anywhere near your place since we left the note,' Hannah insisted.

'Then how come there's a black rabbit sitting munching lettuce in the hutch by my shed at this very minute?'

Helen gasped. 'Are you sure?'

He tutted and picked up his bike. 'If you don't believe me, you'd better come and see.'

'But what about Sorrel?' Hannah wanted to know. She took two steps back towards the gate, then two steps towards Sam.

'Later!' Helen said. She dashed ahead up the lane.

It was Sam's turn to look confused. 'Sorrel's back with me!' he repeated.

So Hannah shook her head as she ran to keep up with his bike until they came to the track leading to his farm. 'No she isn't!' she panted. '*She* definitely is not!'

'Whoops!' Sam braked and stopped. His face turned bright red. 'Did you say *she*?'

As Helen ran on, Hannah nodded. '"She" with a capital "S"! Why didn't you tell us?'

'I didn't think it would make any difference. Who'd be able to tell? Anyway, I never actually said Sorrel was a he, did I?' Sam bit his lip and carried on cycling, more slowly this time. 'How did you find out? Did Miss Wesley spot it?'

'Nope.'

'Your mum?'

'Nope.' She jogged steadily down the track. 'It was when she produced six little baby rabbits that we realised!'

'Wow!' Sam gave another squeal of the brakes. 'You're joking!'

'Nope.' She explained how their dad had discovered the truth about Sorrel the substitute. 'And right now he's phoning Miss Wesley to tell her that the school rabbit isn't a male after all, and that Doveton Junior now has seven rabbits to look after!'

'Uh-oh.' He was lost for words. Instead, he began pedalling hard to catch Helen up, leaving Hannah to trail along on foot.

'Let's get this straight!' Helen glanced over her

shoulder when she felt Sam pull alongside. 'You're saying there's a black rabbit in your hutch?' Though her legs ached, she pounded along the rutted track to see the proof with her own eyes. 'And since we know it can't possibly be Sorrel in there, since she's busy looking after six newborn babies . . . did you know?' She paused to see him nod. '. . . Since it can't be *your* rabbit in your hutch, it stands to reason that it must be Sage!'

Again he nodded. 'That figures.'

'Great!' Helen could hardly wait. 'Never mind how he got in there, as long as he's come back safe, in the end nothing else matters!'

The three of them stood breathless and wind-swept in the yard at Crackpot Farm. They stared in silence at the door of the rabbit hutch swinging open.

'What happened?' Helen wailed. There was no rabbit inside; only straw and an upturned dish of food.

'It wasn't like this when I left, I swear!' Sam cried. He pushed the wire mesh door to and began to search the yard frantically for the rabbit he'd

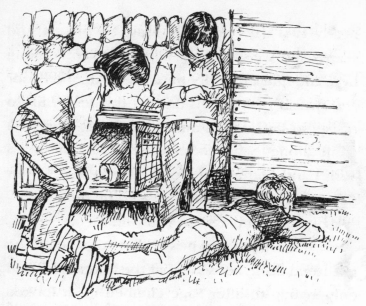

last seen inside the hutch. 'He was in there, you've got to believe me!'

Hannah nodded. 'Did you leave the door locked?' she asked quietly.

'I never checked.' Sam was lying full length on the ground, peering underneath the shed. 'It was a surprise, see. I didn't think.' He wrinkled his nose with disgust. 'Something smells bad under here!'

'Never mind that now.' Hannah was thinking while the other two carried on looking. 'This is what must have happened. Sage has been lost for nearly two days now. He must be hungry and scared, like we said. So he happens to come along here and find a nice dry hutch with an open door and a dish of food inside. It's too tempting to resist, so he hops in and has a feed. Then you come along, Sam, and see him. You think it's Sorrel and you get on your bike to ride to our place and ask what on earth's going on.'

Helen and Sam agreed with the theory so far.

'So what happened next?' Hannah studied the upturned dish. 'Let's say that the hutch door had only swung to after Sage climbed in. It looked closed, but it wasn't latched. Say someone or something came along while Sage was snatching some food . . .'

'And that something scared him,' Helen suggested. She scouted round the back of the bike shed, looking for clues. 'You're right; there's a terrible stink round here.'

Hannah sniffed. 'I can smell it from here.' The scent was strong and bitter. It made her wrinkle her nose and cough. 'Is it some kind of animal?' she wondered.

Slowly Helen emerged from behind the shed.

'You mean, some kind of animal that might have gone up to the hutch and scared Sage off?' She pictured a stealthy shape creeping out from under the shed, silent as a shadow, ready to pounce.

'Maybe.' Hannah wasn't sure. Perhaps they were jumping to too many conclusions.

It was Sam who convinced them. He stood up, his face pale now, brushing stray wisps of straw from his T-shirt. 'I know what this stink is,' he said quietly. 'Once you've smelt it you never forget. Only, I wanted to be sure before I said anything.'

'What is it?' Hannah and Helen said together. They knew before he even gave the answer.

'Fox,' he said: one short, terrifying word. 'That's what crept up on Sage and scared him away!'

Seven

Sam, Hannah and Helen took up the search for the missing rabbit with fresh fear in their hearts.

Half an hour earlier, Sage had been there, large as life, for Sam to see. Now he was gone, hunted down and driven out by a hungry fox. They decided to run to Home Farm to fetch Speckle to pick up the trail for them once more.

'What chance would Sage have against the fox?' Helen whispered as they took a short cut across the fields.

'It depends.' Sam wouldn't say whether or not he thought the rabbit might have escaped.

'But there were no bits of fur . . . or anything!' Hannah's mouth had dried up. She choked and coughed.

'No blood.' Helen realised what she meant and grew more hopeful. 'That's a good thing. It means the fox didn't manage to grab Sage when he was inside the hutch. The dish of food had been kicked over, but that could just have been Sage making a quick run for it.'

'Rabbits move pretty fast,' Sam agreed. 'And they can squeeze down gaps that are too small for a fox.'

The twins nodded and pulled up at the gate to their own farmyard. For a while the shock of what had happened had made them forget about Sorrel and her new family, but the sight of their dad fussing over the hutch reminded them. He looked up when he heard them and put a finger to his lips.

'Ssh! They're all asleep!'

Helen nodded and tiptoed across, while Sam and Hannah went to look for Speckle. By this time their dad had probably got in touch with their teacher and given her the good news. 'What did

Miss Wesley say about the babies?' she asked as she peered into the sleeping compartment.

'What? Oh, she wasn't in. I left a message on her machine for her to ring me when she got back.'

'Did you say what for?' Helen could just see the mass of sleeping babies and the mother rabbit hunched close by.

David Moore shook his head. 'I wanted to keep it as a surprise. I can't wait to hear what she says!'

Me neither, Helen said to herself. But she was glad that he hadn't managed to get through.

'I suppose I could try ringing her again.' He looked at his watch and began to make his way towards the house.

Helen darted ahead of him. 'No, Dad, don't do that!' She waved her arms to stop him from going in.

'Do what?' Hannah had appeared at the door with Speckle and Sam.

'Give Barbara the good news about Sage.' Mr Moore gave a puzzled frown.

'Oh no, don't!' Hannah and Sam repeated in the same breath. Speckle gave a sharp, excited bark.

'Wait till tomorrow,' Helen suggested. 'You said yourself that Sorr . . . Sage would need lots of peace and quiet! We don't want loads of people coming to gawp at her, do we?' She stumbled over the name and mumbled out her feeble reason.

'Barbara Wesley isn't loads of people.' David Moore scratched his head. He looked at their flushed faces. 'I'd like to know what you're up to, I must say.'

'Just don't phone her, Dad, please!' Hannah slid a hand into his and looked up at him, begging him to trust them. 'This is really important!'

He squeezed her hand and smiled. 'How can I resist?'

'So you won't?' Helen insisted. 'That's great! Thanks, Dad!' She was ready to run back to Crackpot Farm to set Speckle on the scent.

As he watched Helen and Speckle go, he shook his head at Hannah and released her hand. 'I must be mad.'

'We'll tell you everything,' she promised. 'Not now, but soon. Don't worry, in the end it'll all make perfect sense!'

* * *

'Dead end!' Sam sighed.

All afternoon they'd followed Sage's trail with Speckle, and now they'd come full circle back to the yard of Crackpot Farm. Still they hadn't found Sage.

Exhausted, Hannah collapsed on her knees beside Speckle. 'Good dog,' she sighed, rewarding him for all his effort. Even if they hadn't succeeded, he'd tried his very best.

'He did pick up the scent loads of times,' Helen said, flopping against the shed. She pushed her hair back from her hot face. 'It's just that it never seemed to lead anywhere.' The determined Border collie had rooted in ditches, cut across fields, gone loping on to the rocky fell, but always come back empty handed. Eventually he'd ranged in smaller and smaller circles until they'd finished up back where they'd started.

Now it was evening; the time when wild rabbits came out of their burrows to feed, when Sage would be hungry too. Hunger might make him risk being seen by the fox, who might be lying in wait for his next opportunity . . .

'I'll keep watch,' Sam promised. He'd worked as hard as Helen and Hannah to find the runaway. 'And I'm sorry all this has happened. I'd like to get Sage back as much as you would.'

'It's not your fault,' Hannah sighed.

'And I didn't know Sorrel was having babies,' he went on, blushing bright red. 'I've only had her for a couple of weeks. We bought her from the pet shop in Nesfield, and they never told us she could already be pregnant.'

'That's OK,' Helen grinned. 'It's funny in a way.'

'Funny!' Sam and Hannah echoed.

'What's funny about trying to explain all this to Miss Wesley?' Hannah insisted. Then a smile crept into the corners of her mouth, her eyes sparkled.

Soon Sam was grinning through his blushes. 'Anyway, I won't give up just because it's going to get dark soon,' he promised again. 'Since Sage knows about the food in this hutch, there's a chance that he'll come back again when it's all quiet. I'll come out and check every so often.'

'Phone us if you see anything.' Helen reminded him. It was time they went home to do their jobs.

'Even the smallest clue!' Hannah insisted. 'Any

tiny sound or movement. Just tell us and we'll bring Speckle across to take a proper look!' She hated to leave, but she knew their mum would be home from work and beginning to worry.

So they trailed home; two figures in jeans and sweatshirts, with muddy shoes and windswept hair, wearily putting one foot after another, following a bedraggled dog down the lane to Home Farm.

'A bite to eat, then a bath and bed for you two!' Mary Moore pronounced the second she set eyes on them.

'What about our jobs?' Helen asked. Chickens, geese, the cat, the dog, the pony . . .

'All done,' their dad said. 'Except Speckle here, and I can soon sort him out. You look worn out, girls. Do as your mum says and have an early night.'

Too weary to resist, they did as they were told. The bath was run and the bubbles frothing, hot chocolate was on the kitchen table, the bedroom curtains were drawn. Then, before they knew it they were in clean pyjamas, snuggled in bed, with Speckle already snoozing by the door.

'Tomorrow's the day for explanations,

remember!' Their dad looked in on them before he turned out the light.

Helen turned and sighed. Hannah hitched her duvet tighter under her chin.

'The mystery is about to be unravelled!'

Flick. The light went out, his teasing words floated in the dark. Then all was quiet.

'I'm never going to get to sleep!' Hannah murmured. She thought of the fox that was supposed to be so strong and daring. The stink of him under Sam's shed, the hutch door hanging open.

'Me neither.' Helen couldn't get Sage out of her mind. So small and black and helpless. So lost.

Within minutes the exhausted girls were fast asleep.

They woke with the dawn, sitting upright in bed, wide awake, listening.

'Did you hear that?' Helen whispered.

Hannah nodded. 'It was Speckle growling.'

Together they slipped out of bed and crept to the window where the dog stood, ears pricked, the hackles at the back of his neck raised.

'What is it, Speckle?' Hannah slid the curtain open and peered out. The chestnut tree rustled in the deep, early morning silence.

'What did you hear?' Helen bent to whisper to him, gazing into his eager face.

The dog dipped out of her reach and trotted to the bedroom door. He came back, did it again.

'He wants us to go with him!' she hissed.

'Quick, I think I saw something move down there!' Hannah let the curtain drop and ran to the door. It had been too shadowy and dim to make out what it was. A currant bush growing against the wall had rustled, a shape had crept out.

They let Speckle out of the room and followed him downstairs in their bare feet. Along the narrow hallway, out through the front door. The chill, damp air hit them and they shivered.

Speckle crouched low to the ground and growled.

'Shh!' Hannah warned. She led him quietly to the bush where she'd seen the shadow move.

And now the hairs at the back of Helen and Hannah's own necks began to prickle. Their bare arms were covered in goosebumps as they crept with Speckle across the yard.

Hannah peered under the bush. 'Nothing!' Whatever it was must have gone. She loosened her grip on Speckle's collar and sighed.

Helen sniffed the air. The scent caught in the back of her throat.

Then Hannah saw a flash of white in the grey dawn light. It moved along the wall-top under the chestnut tree as if it was floating through the shadows: the tip of an animal's tail. An animal the same size as Speckle, but brownish-red when they made out the sturdy body attached to the white tip of the tail. An animal with a long, cruel snout and bared teeth as it turned from the rabbit hutch to snarl a warning at the dog.

The fox! Hannah drew back as Speckle leaped forward. Helen tried to stop him, but he brushed past. The fox on the wall faced the dog on the ground, fangs bared ready to fight for its supper.

'Mum, Dad! Come quick!' Hannah's voice split the air. She yelled until the light in their bedroom went on and the curtain flew open. 'A fox is attacking Speckle. Come quick!'

Snarling, the fox flew from the wall on to the ground and hurled itself at the dog. The two animals locked together, rolling and snapping across the yard. They were up on their feet, crouching and darting, then snarling and charging again as the door of the house opened and David Moore came out armed with a broom.

'Watch out, Speckle!' Helen cried.

The dog pulled free and rolled away.

Their dad lunged forward, wielding the broom's stiff bristles in the fox's face. The creature yelped and shot backwards, cowering away from the broom.

David Moore shouted. 'Go on, haah! Get away! Go on, shoo!' He jabbed at the fox to corner it and give Speckle time to recover.

The dog got up and limped towards the rabbit hutch. His bark ripped through the air, down the valley and up the fell.

'Keep him there, Dad!' Shaking with terror, Hannah realised that they had the fox trapped. If her father could get him into the far corner of the yard, they could surround him and trap him somehow. 'A box! We need a box!' she yelled to her mum, standing at the door in her dark red dressing-gown.

It all happened in seconds: the fight, the cornering. As David Moore jabbed the creature tighter into the corner and Speckle went on barking, the fox saw that the battle was lost. He whipped himself round in a flurry of snarls and bushy tail, crouched and sprang away from the broom, into the air and over the wall. One instant he was there and trapped; the next he was gone.

'Too late,' Helen said as her mum came running out with a big wooden crate. The corner was empty, the fox was fleeing across the fields.

Still Speckle barked from under the chestnut tree. They turned and were struck dumb. They saw that the fox had been at work on the rabbit hutch long before the twins woke up. He'd scratched with his sharp claws and chewed with his pointed teeth until he'd worn a hole in the wiremesh front.

'Where's the rabbit?' Mary Moore gasped, lifting the lid of the sleeping compartment.

'Gone!' David Moore shook his head.

Helen and Hannah shut their eyes and groaned.

Jenny Oldfield

'She must have been scared out of her wits,' the twins' mum murmured as she stared in at the abandoned litter of baby rabbits asleep in the nest.

Eight

'This is the worst thing that could happen!' Hannah cried. Her hand trembled as she tried to pick up the phone to ring Sam Lawson.

'Wait. Calm down.' Mary Moore took it from her. 'Sam will still be in bed. It's only six o'clock, and it's Sunday.'

'But we have to tell him what's happened!' There were tears in Helen's eyes too. This was a disaster. Now there was a fox, *two* missing rabbits and a nestful of orphans.

'How about telling us first?' David Moore said gently. He sat them down at the table and waited.

Helen stared down at her hands. Where should they begin?

But Hannah was so upset that the words tumbled out. 'Sage isn't really Sage; she's Sorrel. And Sage isn't a she, he's a he. And Sorrel is the one who just ran away from the fox. We never found Sage after he escaped from the run. We only pretended we did. And Sorrel belongs to Sam. She was just pretending to be Sage. And then she went and had babies. And now they've both gone, and the fox has probably eaten them both!' Hot tears ran down her cheeks as she came to the end of the confession.

'Whoa!' David Moore put his hands up. 'You lost me around about the point where Sage wasn't really Sage but Sorrel.'

The twins' mum sat down quietly to figure it out. 'I think I see what you're saying. But my question is *why*? Why go to all this trouble of getting a substitute rabbit?'

'We didn't want to let Miss Wesley down,' Helen whispered. She hung her head and stared at the patterns of wood grain on the table.

'We were sure we'd be able to find Sage and

put him back in his hutch before anyone found out,' Hannah added. 'But even Speckle couldn't track him down.'

'And then the fox showed up.' Helen's top lip trembled.

'And now the fox has probably eaten them both, and everything's gone completely wrong!' Hannah wailed again.

'OK, we don't know that for certain. What we need to do is think.' Mary Moore had got dressed as soon as they came back into the house. Now she twisted her long dark hair on top of her head, ready for action. 'How long have we got before the baby rabbits need their mother back for their next feed?' she asked.

'Not long.' David Moore could only guess. 'A few hours at the most.'

'Then would they starve?' Hannah whispered.

He nodded. 'They're very young. They need their mother with them to keep them warm and fed.'

'Poor things,' Helen murmured. 'And poor Sorrel.' The fox's face must have appeared on the other side of the wire netting in the dim dawn light, his teeth and claws must have wrenched that hole. The mother rabbit had seized her only chance and fled in terror.

'I reckon she wouldn't just abandon those babies,' Hannah said. She was beginning to get over the shock and start to think. 'Imagine; a vicious fox appears and rips his way in. What can she do? She can stay and fight, but he's mean and cruel, and she's bound to lose. She and her babies will all die. Or she can draw him away from the hutch before he has chance to get at the nest.'

'A sort of decoy?' Helen asked.

She nodded. 'If she makes the fox chase her, then he can't attack the babies. So I reckon that's what she did.'

'And Speckle heard the racket and warned us just as the fox had jumped on to the wall to follow Sorrel?' Helen nodded. 'That ruined his plan; he had to stay and deal with our brave dog instead of chasing the rabbit!'

'Which means that Sorrel got away and might ﾀe back!' Hannah saw that all wasn't lost.

ﾀt!' All this time their dad had listened, but

88

now he stepped in. 'Aren't you forgetting something?'

'What?' they chimed.

'The fox got away too, remember.'

'He could be lurking in the field right now, or following this heroic mother rabbit you've been describing.' Their mum didn't want them to raise their hopes too high either.

The twins nodded. It was like being on a roller-coaster; plunging, then slowly crawling up a slope, only to plunge again into despair.

The sudden ringing of the phone made them all jump. Hannah was nearest. Her hand shook once more as she picked it up.

'It's a bit early, isn't it?' David Moore frowned.

'Who can it be?' Mary wondered.

'Shh!' Hannah could hear a voice gabbling on the other end of the phone. 'Sam, is that you?'

'Yes, it's me. Listen; this is amazing! You've got to get here quick. I couldn't believe it when I went to check the hutch like I said I would.'

'When?' She could hardly make sense of what he was trying to say.

'Just now. I woke up, saw it was light, and went down to take a look.'

'And what did you see?' *A black rabbit!* she prayed. *Please say you've seen Sorrel!*

'A fox!' he gasped. 'Standing on top of the wall!'

Hannah groaned and crumpled forward, while Helen grabbed the phone from her.

'Sam, it's me, Helen! Tell me what you've just told Hannah, quick!' It was bad news, she could tell.

'I've seen the fox. He was kind of lifting his head and barking. Creepy! But listen, I hadn't finished.' He gabbled again, to make sure he told the whole story. 'When I went over to try and scare him off, I found out why he'd come back in the first place! There he was, standing guard over the hutch, and guess who was inside!'

'Tell me!' Helen held her breath. There could be two answers she could think of; Sorrel or Sage. She made him spell it out.

'Not one, but two black rabbits! They're here at Crackpot Farm. Helen, it's Sorrel and Sage; e come back!'

* * *

The Moores jumped into the car with Speckle and drove over to the Lawsons' farm. Within five minutes of Sam's phone call they were there. But once more the fox was gone and the hutch was empty. So near, and yet so far.

'What happened this time?' Hannah demanded. She'd been certain that they would get there in time, that they would soon be carrying Sorrel back to her babies, locking Sage safely inside his hutch, ready to take him back to school.

Sam shook his head. 'Sorry. I only let them out of my sight while I phoned you, but when I came back there was no sign of any of them!' He looked upset, standing beside his mother, who had got up to see what all the fuss was about.

'It's not your fault,' Mary Moore told him. 'And anyway, this time they probably can't have got very far.' She set about organising a search party. 'You kids stick together with Speckle and search the barn and the farmyard. We grown-ups will tackle the fields leading down to the lane. Come on, what are we waiting for?'

Helen sprang into action. 'We need the box in case we corner the fox again!'

David Moore fetched the wooden crate from the boot of the car and placed it by the farmyard gate. 'One box!' he announced.

'And we need something to tempt Sorrel and Sage out of hiding with!' Hannah knew it would have to be a tasty treat to overcome their fear.

'Carrots!' Sam produced some from his pocket. 'I already thought of that.'

'Ready?' Mary Moore asked.

They nodded, wished each other luck and set off in different directions.

First, Helen checked the inside of Sam's rabbit hutch. Then she looked underneath the bike shed and crept along the narrow passage between the shed and the wall, peering into every crevice and under every mossy stone.

Meanwhile, Hannah took Speckle, let him smell the hutch then set him loose in the yard, telling him to track down rabbit. The dog sniffed busily, then quickly led her towards the barn.

'This way!' Hannah hissed at Sam and Helen. In the background she could see the three grown-
_ing out across the fields. She turned back
_e, to find him sniffing up against the

closed door, then poking his nose through a gap between the ground and the worn wooden planks. 'What do you think?' she whispered.

Sam shook his head. 'Too small.' The hole was hardly big enough to get a hand through.

Helen watched Speckle push his long nose under the door. She nodded. 'Speckle knows what he's doing. He's definitely telling us that this is the way Sorrel and Sage came!'

'How do we get in?' Hannah pushed at the huge, bolted door.

'Through here.' Sam led them round the far side of the barn and in through a small door.

As Helen and Hannah followed him into the dark, high space, Speckle dashed ahead and disappeared behind a stack of bales of straw.

'Has anyone got a torch?' Helen whispered. The barn seemed to be full of rustles and creaks that she couldn't make out. Overhead she was sure she heard the beating of wings; an owl or a bat? She shivered and hunched her shoulders. What other creatures lurked here in the dark?

'I have.' Sam produced one from his pocket and turned on the light. It flashed over the bales, up towards the roof, catching specks of dust and wisps of straw in its yellow beam.

Gradually Hannah's eyes grew used to the darkness all around. 'Let's follow Speckle,' she suggested. 'And keep really quiet. If the rabbits are in here, we don't want to scare them off.'

Sam shone the light on one side of the stack, picking out a way through. 'Come on!' He was about to lead on when Helen stopped him.

'What's that?' She pointed to a white patch on the ground and asked Sam to hold the torch steady. Then she crept forward.

Hannah came and crouched beside her. She groaned. There on the floor of the barn was a small heap of feathers.

'Do you think the fox did this?' Gingerly Helen reached out a hand to touch the soft white down. Beyond the heap was a scattering of more feathers and a speck or two of fresh, wet blood.

Sam shone the torch closer and nodded. 'Probably a pigeon,' he whispered.

'It means he got in here as well as Sorrel and fact, he must still be here in the barn, om us.' Hannah backed off from the remains of the fox's latest meal. 'He's probably watching us!'

'Wait here. I'll fetch the crate!' Before the twins could object, Sam turned and ran, taking the torch with him.

In the darkness, from behind the bales of straw, they heard Speckle scratch and whine. To Helen it meant that the dog had found something important. So she began to scramble over the nearest bales, feeling her way, until she came to the top of the stack. 'Are you coming?' she whispered back down to Hannah.

'I'll squeeze through this gap and meet you at the far side,' she answered, picking her way past the scattered feathers. Ahead, she could see slits of daylight from the gaps in the old wooden doors. They lit Speckle, who gave a sharp yap when he saw her. 'What is it?' she urged.

He scratched at the floor and whined again.

Hannah saw him in silhouette, recognised the raised hackles, realised that his bark was a warning. To her? Or to a hidden enemy? A growl came from deep in his throat as he pawed the floor.

And then she caught the smell. The same sharp stink. And the glint of an eye from behind a tower of straw bales, a fierce amber eye glaring at her . . . The fox was here, just as they'd thought. And now Speckle had him trapped.

'Helen, come quick!' Looking round in the gloom, she saw a long-handled rake propped against a wall. She seized it and crept forwards, holding it up like a javelin. She heard Helen slide down the stack of bales behind her and Sam's footsteps echoing as he ran back with the crate.

There was a flash of white fangs, a snap of strong jaws as the fox leaped out of its corner. Speckle stood his ground. Hannah thrust the rake forwards and down. The metal prongs rammed against the stone floor, blocking the fox's path before he reached the steadfast dog.

'Here, Sam! Bring the box!' Helen yelled for help as she landed beside her sister.

Hannah drove the snarling creature back into the corner. How long could she keep him cowering there?

Sam came and dumped the crate on the ground, knocking bales and sending them flying. They

tumbled and rolled, but the crate was in place, one end open, ready for Hannah to drive the fox out of the corner and into the box.

Hannah held her breath. The fox had her in its gaze. It crouched and snarled, ears laid flat, tail between its legs. She prodded again with the rake, steering it out of its corner towards the box.

'Careful!' Helen cried. The fox had tried to leap over the rake and bolt for freedom, but Hannah's quick reaction stopped him. Again she jabbed and steered.

The fox sidled away from the metal prongs,

snapping and darting its head.

'Nearly!' Helen whispered. It was inches away from the open crate, edging sideways into it.

'Yes!' Sam cried. As Hannah finally drove the creature into the crate, he pounced. *Slam!* The lid flew shut with a kick. He braced his foot against it and watched the fox cower in defeat.

Nine

'No wonder he scared the living daylights out of Sage and Sorrel!' David Moore peered inside the crate at the gleaming amber eyes of the trapped fox.

'Speckle did brilliantly to stand up to him,' Mrs Lawson said. 'And quick thinking from you three too.' She gave credit where it was due, to Sam, Hannah and Helen.

Rapidly the twins pleaded with Sam's mum not to have the captured fox shot, but to put him in the Land-Rover and drive him far up the fell, away from the farms and villages.

'To a wild spot up on one of the high passes,' she promised. 'I'll let him go in an area where he can't do any more harm to people's pets and livestock.'

Helen watched the grown-ups carry the fox to the car. 'That's fair,' she murmured to the others. 'After all, when the fox came after the rabbits, he was only doing what he was born to do.'

'We just don't want him to do it round here, that's all,' Hannah agreed. Until Mrs Lawson drove off with the crate, she wouldn't breathe easily.

'OK, relax,' the twins' dad said as they waved the car off up the track. 'Public enemy number one is on his way out of here. Let's go and give the all-clear!'

'He means, we'd better let everyone know the good news,' Mrs Moore explained. 'The whole neighbourhood has been anxious about that fox these last few days. We should ring Fred Hunt and Luke Martin. They'll be able to pass the message on for us.' She was getting into the car, ready to drive back to Home Farm.

'We'll stay here,' Hannah decided.

'To look for Sage and Sorrel,' Helen added.

'We can't relax . . .'

'. . . Until we find them.'

'We reckon they're still . . .'

'. . . In the barn.' Helen glanced over her shoulder at the closed doors.

Their mum and dad nodded and told them to be careful. 'Fingers crossed!' Mary Moore said.

'Let's go!' Sam went first, torch at the ready, followed by Speckle, Hannah and Helen.

'OK now; rabbits!' Helen hissed, crouching down to the dog's level as they entered the barn. 'Find them, Speckle!'

Two black rabbits in a dark barn. Two scared, confused pets driven to their wits' ends by a pair of amber eyes and a set of sharp teeth. This seemed like the very last chance to find them and take them safely home.

'Where do we start?' Sam whispered. He shone the fading torch up the stack of pale straw bales, flicked it across the beams that held up the roof and down the rough stone wall at the far side.

'We wait for Speckle,' Hannah murmured. She watched him sniff at the heap of white feathers, turn away, sniff again, then begin to climb the main stack of bales. Soon he was three metres above ground and still steadily climbing.

Helen looked at Hannah. 'What do we do now?'

'Follow him.' There were steps up the stack, made by the way the Lawsons had piled the square bales roof-high. 'If we can see where he is!' she added.

The torch beam was by now so weak that it hardly gave any light. 'Sorry!' Sam shook the torch and shrugged. 'It's the batteries.'

So they had to climb without it, clambering from bale to bale, until they too were a long way from the ground, up amongst the old wooden beams where the owls and the bats roosted.

'Yuck!' Helen brushed a filmy cobweb from her cheek. She shuddered as she glanced down. 'I hope Speckle knows what he's doing!'

'He does, look!' Hannah pointed to the very top of the stack, where the dog stood patiently waiting. He'd led them as far as he could; after this it would be up to them.

'Where, Speckle?' Helen steeled herself to climb the last row of bales. Then she was on the top of the stack beside him, peering up into the roof. 'Where are they?'

The dog reared up and put his front paws on the nearest beam. It ran on a level from one side of the barn to the other; a massive timber to support the roof beams. Helen looked along it. Surely Sage and Sorrel hadn't scrambled along there in their panic to get away from the fox?

'Oh no!' They'd done just that. Sam saw them hunched at the far end of the beam. He gasped and pointed.

They were perched like tight-rope walkers in the middle of nowhere. Huddled together on the beam, they sat still as statues. With a drop of ten metres to the floor below, they'd chosen the only hiding place in the whole barn where the fox might not be able to follow.

'What now?' Hannah felt herself go dizzy at the sight of the rabbits.

'I'll crawl along to fetch them!' Helen didn't hesitate.

'No, it's too dangerous!' Sam tried to stand in her way. 'It's not worth it, Helen!'

She stared him out. 'Give me one of the carrots,'

she said quietly. 'Maybe I won't have to crawl very far once they smell this.'

'Helen, be careful!' Hannah held Speckle's collar to hold him back. Then she turned to Sam. 'Will you hang on to Speckle for me? I'm going to follow her.'

'Not you too!' He protested, but he knew there was no stopping them.

'Yes. If Helen manages to tempt one of the rabbits along the beam, she's going to need someone behind her so she can pass it on. I'll bring the first one back here while she goes for the second.' She had it clearly planned, forgetting the danger and concentrating instead on how they were going to rescue Sage and Sorrel from their terrifying ordeal.

So they set off, inch by inch. First Helen tested the beam, then sat astride it. Then she lay flat with her arms hugging it and hauled herself along. Hannah nodded and copied.

'Don't look down!' Helen warned. She'd just made that mistake. Way below, the ground swam dizzily.

Hannah kept her eyes on the beam. With Sage

and Sorrel firmly in her sights she knew she could keep going. 'Use the carrot!' she whispered, when they were halfway across. 'Make them come towards us!'

Holding on to the beam with one hand, Helen drew the carrot out of her pocket. She saw the nearest rabbit prick up his ears and sniff. Come *on!* she urged silently, not moving a muscle in case she scared him off.

Good, good! Hannah said under her breath. She too froze on the spot.

The first rabbit shifted, then stood up. He bobbed his head towards the carrot, took a first step in their direction. Was it safe? Should they trust these people? He seemed to turn and check with the second rabbit. Then slowly, warily, they both edged forward.

Helen held the carrot at arm's length. It's working! Now hold steady. Don't move! Another few hops along the beam and the rabbits would be within reach.

'Now!' Hannah whispered.

Helen felt the rabbit take the bait. She lunged forward and swept him up in her arms. He struggled, kicking and scratching with all his might. She held tight, swung him round towards Hannah, as the second rabbit took fright and began to charge at them.

Hannah reacted like lightning, ready to take one rabbit from Helen. She snatched him to her, watched Helen reach for the second runaway, gasped with relief as he too charged straight along the beam into her arms.

'Brilliant!' Sam stood on the top of the stack of bales and cheered. Speckle barked. Down below, the big doors were flung wide open. The barn was flooded with light.

The twins clutched the rabbits close to them, swung their legs over the beam and turned. Still they couldn't relax. The way back was even more difficult; one-handed with a small, struggling creature to take care of.

'Goodness!' Mary Moore's shocked voice called out from below.

'It's OK, we can make it!' Hannah called. Only a couple of metres to go. She felt the rabbit kick and struggle, but she kept going until she reached the bales. Then she swung her leg over the beam, launched herself into the air and slid on to the mountain of straw; sliding, sliding with the rabbit clutched to her until she reached the ground.

'Nearly . . . nearly!' Helen and her rabbit edged back to safety. She swung herself off the beam and slid on the slippery straw; bumping and skidding to Hannah's side.

They sat on a cushion of pale straw. It was in their hair, scratching their arms and legs. Speckle and Sam tumbled down the stack after them. Hannah and Helen held up their rabbits to show the others. Victory!

'. . . Just one problem,' David Moore said as he helped the twins to stand and brushed them down. 'Which rabbit is which?'

Helen looked at her coal-black rabbit. His eyes shone like glass buttons, his pink ears flicked. 'This is Sorrel!' she declared.

Hannah frowned and studied her rabbit's long whiskers and soft black fur. 'No, *this* is Sorrel!' She felt absolutely sure.

'Isn't *that* one Sage?' Sam pointed to Hannah's rabbit.

'I thought *that* one was the school rabbit!' Mary

Moore chose the runaway nestled in Helen's arms.

'No . . . *that* one . . . *this* one . . . *that* one . . .!'

There was silence as the sun shone in on the confused group.

Helen sat her rabbit alongside Hannah's and shook her head. The twin rabbits got over the fuss and began to munch the carrot she'd given them. *Chew-chew-chew, munch-munch* in perfect harmony.

Hannah stared wide-eyed. 'How will we ever know?'

Ten

Sage the school rabbit, Sorrel the substitute. Which one was which?

As they drove down the lane to Home Farm, Hannah and Helen nervously cuddled a rabbit each.

'We could ask Sally Freeman,' Mary Moore suggested from the front seat. She glanced over her shoulder at Sam and the twins fidgeting on the back seat.

Mrs Freeman was the local vet.

'She's away for half-term.' Hannah knew that the whole Freeman family had gone on holiday.

'OK, so we could ask someone like Fred Hunt.' This was their dad's idea. He was trying to keep a smile off his face as he drove along. 'An old farmer is bound to know the difference!'

'Too embarrassing!' Helen cried. She stroked her rabbit and thought hard.

'I know!' Sam suddenly came up with the solution as they reached the twins' house. 'Come on, bring them both with you!' He sped across to the ledge under the chestnut tree where the two hutches sat side by side. 'Which one has the babies inside?' he demanded.

'This one.' Hannah pointed to the home-made hutch where Sorrel had given birth.

'So, this is gonna be easy!' He nodded and opened the wiremesh door. 'Put your rabbit in first, Hannah. See what happens.'

Hannah saw what he was getting at. 'You mean, if this is Sorrel, she'll make her way straight to the sleeping compartment to take care of the babies?' She stroked her rabbit's long ears, then let it sniff at the straw lining the floor of the hutch.

'Yep. Go on, do it!'

So, gently, nervously Hannah put the rabbit into

the hutch. It landed with a small thump and took one hop. It sniffed at the ramp leading to the compartment where the six babies lay, took half a step up the slope.

'Yes!' Hannah whispered. 'This one must be the mother!'

'No!' Helen saw the rabbit turn and bob down the ramp. It snuffled and wrinkled its black nose, sitting up on its hind legs, front paws dangling. Carrot! Dried oats, apple. It smelt food. And food was more interesting to a male rabbit than babies asleep. In a flash it bounded across the hutch to the feeding dish and began to chomp happily.

'That's Sage!' Sam said with a grin.

'So this must be Sorrel!' Helen gave her own rabbit a farewell stroke, then put her into the hutch.

And this time there was no mistake. The female rabbit didn't hesitate. Up the ramp she scurried and into the quiet sleeping compartment. As Sage stuffed his face and drank his fill, Sorrel sat in the dark and suckled her hungry babies.

Hammer, hammer, hammer! Thud-ouch, thud-

thud-ouch!' David Moore was at work once more.

Hannah and Helen relaxed in the sun with Speckle. They kept an eye on Sage as he bobbed up and down the run in Solo's field. It was Wednesday afternoon, and he'd spent all day nibbling dandelion leaves and looking for a way out.

'Oh no, you don't!' Helen laughed as the cheeky rabbit scratched at the earth. 'I know you're good at burrowing, but we're not going to let you escape again!'

'You'd think he'd have learned his lesson,' Hannah murmured. 'After the frights with the fox, you'd think he'd never want to leave the hutch ever again!' For three whole days there had been no word of the terror of Doveton. He'd taken to the wilds, to roam the high hills.

'Anyway, tomorrow it's back to school,' Helen reminded her. They would drive Sage back to his permanent home under Miss Wesley's careful eye.

'Ugh!' Hannah groaned. 'School!' Where had the week's holiday gone?

'There; finished!' Their dad dropped his hammer and stood up straight. 'What do you think?'

The twins went to inspect his handiwork. They walked along a neat row of small wooden houses, trying out the wiremesh doors, checking the catches.

'Six rabbit hutches all ready and waiting!' he said proudly.

'They're great, Dad!' Helen was impressed. The corners were all square, the roofs watertight. His DIY was definitely improving.

'Practice makes perfect!' he said, tapping the nearest one before sauntering off for a tea break.

'Sorrel's babies will love them!' Hannah agreed. 'When they're big enough to leave their mum.' In a few weeks' time they would all be needing homes of their own.

'Here comes Sam.' Helen had spotted the fair haired figure riding his bike down the lane. Since the weekend rescue he'd spent most of his time at Home Farm helping to look after the rabbits.

'How are they?' he asked as he curved into the yard and skidded to a halt. He flung the bike to the ground and made straight for Sorrel's hutch.

'If you mean the babies, they're all doing well.' Helen lifted the lid to show him. Inside the snug nest, six downy pink rabbits slept.

'Where's Sorrel?'

'Having a rest. She's allowed to, isn't she?' Helen showed him the mother rabbit sitting quietly in the next door hutch. 'We're feeding her up and giving her extra milk. Don't worry, she's OK.'

They peered in at her to make sure, smiled as she shook her whiskers at them, turned her back and went on grooming.

'Now, about these hutches . . .' David Moore came out of the house, mug in hand.

The twins and Sam left Sorrel in peace and went to join him.

'. . . They all need a coat of varnish. Who's going to volunteer?'

'Me! Me! Me!' Three brushes and three pots of clear waterproof varnish later, they were all at work.

''Course, it'll be weeks before we can move Sorrel back to Crackpot Farm,' Hannah reminded Sam. She was loving looking after the mother rabbit and her family at Home Farm.

'That's fine.' Sam slapped on the varnish, *slip-slop*.

'Watch it!' Helen warned. She caught the spray from his brush. 'It'll probably be the long summer holidays before they can be moved.' Why didn't he argue and demand to have Sorrel back at Crackpot Farm?

'I know. That's OK.' He whistled as he worked.

Helen glanced at Hannah and shrugged. What had come over Sam? Why wasn't he being rude and horrible?

'As long as the baby rabbits grow up big and strong, I don't mind how long I have to wait.' He dipped his brush into the pot and painted happily.

Hannah frowned. She'd spotted a possible problem. 'Is your mum going to let you keep all six?'

'Nope.' He sprayed varnish all over the place. 'She says I can't keep any of them. Sorrel's enough of a handful as it is.'

'Don't you care?' Helen knew she would have been heartbroken.

Hannah suspected from the look on his face that Sam Lawson had a plan. 'What are you going to do with them if you can't keep them?'

'Sell them.' The answer came out of the blue.

'Sell them!' the twins cried. Of course; this was more like the Sam they knew.

'Yep; look.' He dropped his brush in the pot and drew out a smudged, creased card from his pocket. 'I made up an advert already. What do you think?'

'Wanted: Good Homes', they read in big print. 'Baby Dutch Dwarf Rabbits For Sale!' Underneath, in smaller letters, Sam had added the words, 'Brand new rabbit hutches also for sale.'

They stared at the hutches they were varnishing, looked up and glared. 'You might have asked us first!'

'Well!' Sam blushed. 'I knew you'd want me to find good homes for the babies. And I can't sell them without hutches. And . . . well, I didn't think your dad would mind!'

The sun bathed the classroom in bright, warm light as Hannah and Helen put Sage's hutch on to Miss Wesley's desk first thing on Thursday morning.

Mark Wood, Lorna Milne and the rest crowded round to greet the school rabbit.

'Now sit down, everyone!' The teacher called for order. 'You can all see Sage from your desks. That's better!'

The class did as they were told. Hannah and Helen went to sit at the back, next to Mark and Sam.

Sage sat quietly, tilting his head from side to side, looking out at the rows of bright faces.

'Aah, isn't he sweet!'

'Look at his little furry face!'

'Miss, he's grown!'

'No, he hasn't. He's just the same!'

Once more Miss Wesley quietened them. 'It's nice to have him back, isn't it? And I think we should thank Hannah and Helen for the wonderful job they did in looking after Sage.' She smiled across the rows of faces which all turned to look at them as she spoke.

Helen felt herself grow hot and red. Hannah ducked her head.

'We're very grateful to you both,' the teacher went on sweetly. 'And I'm sure we're all wondering what sort of week Sage has had with you at Home Farm. Would you like to tell us any special adventures?'

All eyes were fixed on them. In the seat beside Helen, Sam sniggered.

She kicked him hard under the desk. 'Don't you dare!'

'No, Miss!' Hannah whispered. She knew it was best to keep quiet about the runaway rabbit. For how could she ever begin to explain the story of Sorrel the substitute?

SKYE THE CHAMPION
Home Farm Twins 13

Jenny Oldfield

Meet Helen and Hannah. They're identical twins – and mad about the animals on their Lake District farm!

When their dad is involved in a car accident, the twins are glad he's not hurt. But the trailer he hit was carrying a prize highland cow and her calf – and the young calf is injured. Will the angry owner sue Mr Moore? Can Helen and Hannah find a way to take the now unwanted calf off his hands?

SUGAR & SPICE THE PICKPOCKETS
Home Farm Twins 14

Jenny Oldfield

Meet Helen and Hannah. They're identical twins – and mad about the animals on their Lake District farm!

Two squirrels invade the loft of the local shop and cause a row in Doveton. Should they be left alone or got rid of? When small items vanish from the shop, it seems as though the squirrels' days are numbered. But Hannah and Helen suspect that someone or something else is beyond the thefts – and they plan to investigate!

SOPHIE THE SHOW-OFF
Home Farm Twins 15

Jenny Oldfield

Meet Helen and Hannah. They're identical twins – and mad about the animals on their Lake District farm!

Sophie's a rescue cat with a habit of showing off – and it's causing all sorts of problems! Parading by the lake in front of tourists, she slips off the ferry rail; stalking doves on the shop roof, she nearly takes a tumble. Luckily for her, the twins are on hand to help. But now Sophie plans to put in an appearance at the local cricket match! Can Helen and Hannah stop her?

HOME FARM TWINS
Jenny Oldfield

66127 5	Speckle The Stray	£3.50	❏
66128 3	Sinbad The Runaway	£3.50	❏
66129 1	Solo The Homeless	£3.50	❏
66130 5	Susie The Orphan	£3.50	❏
66131 3	Spike The Tramp	£3.50	❏
66132 1	Snip and Snap The Truants	£3.50	❏
68990 0	Sunny The Hero	£3.50	❏
68991 9	Socks The Survivor	£3.50	❏
68992 7	Stevie The Rebel	£3.50	❏
68993 5	Samson The Giant	£3.50	❏
69983 3	Sultan The Patient	£3.50	❏
69984 1	Sorrel The Substitute	£3.50	❏
69985 X	Skye The Champion	£3.50	❏

All Hodder Children's books are available at your local bookshop, or can be ordered direct from the publisher. Just tick the titles you would like and complete the details below. Prices and availability are subject to change without prior notice.

Please enclose a cheque or postal order made payable to *Bookpoint Ltd*, and send to: Hodder Children's Books, 39 Milton Park, Abingdon, OXON OX14 4TD, UK.
Email Address: orders@bookpoint.co.uk

If you would prefer to pay by credit card, our call centre team would be delighted to take your order by telephone. Our direct line *01235 400414* (lines open 9.00 am–6.00 pm Monday to Saturday, 24 hour message answering service). Alternatively you can send a fax on *01235 400454*.

TITLE		FIRST NAME		SURNAME	

ADDRESS	

DAYTIME TEL:		POST CODE	

If you would prefer to pay by credit card, please complete:
Please debit my Visa/Access/Diner's Card/American Express (delete as applicable) card no:

Signature .... Expiry Date: ....

If you would NOT like to receive further information on our products please tick the box. ❏